AUDREY'S TREE HOUSE

by Jenny Hughes

illustrated by Jonathan Bentley

Scholastic Inc.

"Your house is getting too small for me,"
said Audrey one morning.

"You do look much bigger than you did yesterday," said Dad. "But where will you go?"

"I haven't decided yet," said Audrey.

So Dad and Audrey went outside to look.

"How about here?" said Dad.

"Way too small," said Audrey.

"What about here?"
asked Dad.

"It's far too big,"
said Audrey.

"Or here?"

"It's too crowded," Audrey said.
"Let's build a house up there!"

"It's very high," said Dad.

"Almost as high as the sky," said Audrey.
"But I'm bigger than I was yesterday."

So Audrey and her dad went to see what they could find.

"First I'll need a staircase," said Audrey.
"With a banister, so I can slide from the top."

Dad built a staircase.

"And somewhere I can play,
with a bathtub for snorkeling."

Dad built a place to play.

"And somewhere to sip tea, please," said Audrey.
"And a place to hide the dirty cups."

Dad made somewhere
to sip tea.

"A blue bed would be nice," said Audrey.
"So I can keep my secrets underneath."

Dad made a bed.

"Now I need a chair for every guest."

Dad made chairs.

"And don't forget a stove so I can make cupcakes
and lick the bowl clean."

Dad made a stove.

"It's a very high house," said Dad.

"Thank you very much," said Audrey.
"It's almost as high as the sky."

"Well, good night, my darling,"
said Dad as he tidied his tools.
"Don't stay up late."

Audrey's tummy turned over.

"I don't have my fluffy blanket," she said.

"You can borrow my sweater," said Dad
as he walked down the staircase.

Audrey sniffed.

"I think I've caught a cold," she said.
"I might sneeze the leaves off the tree."

Dad headed up the path. "You can rake them up
in the morning," he said.

Audrey's knees trembled.

"But I've eaten the cupcakes," she said.
"My tummy might grumble and wake up the birds."

"Birds don't mind waking up early," said Dad
as he passed the pond.

"But what if it rains during the night?" Audrey said.
"I might wash away in a flood!"

"I know where there's a staircase," said Dad.

"Do you?" said Audrey.

"It leads to a place safe and warm," said Dad.

"Does it?" said Audrey.

"There's soup for two and two snug beds.
You can always come home with me."

"Are you sure?" asked Audrey.

"Very sure," said Dad.

"Even if I'm bigger than I was yesterday?" said Audrey.

"Even if you're twice as big as you were yesterday," said Dad.

"For as long as I like?" asked Audrey.

"Even longer," said Dad.

Audrey ran up the path, and together
they climbed the steps to the house,
which wasn't too small at all.

For Ivy, Freya, Katie, and Margrete—J.H.
For Ruby—J.B.

First published in Australia by Little Hare Books, an imprint of Hardie Grant Egmont, in 2014, under the title *A House of Her Own.*

ISBN 978-0-545-81405-8

10 9 8 7 6 5 4 3 2 1   15 16 17 18 19

Printed in the U.S.A. 40

This edition first printing, January 2015

The illustrations were created using watercolors, pencil, and scanned textures.